AF227944

Madness Heart Press
2006 Idlewilde Run Dr.
Austin, Texas 78744

Cover provided by SRS Cinema LLC

First Edition
ISBN: 978-1-967517-19-0
www.madnessheart.press

OUIJA SLUMBER PARTY

Edward Lee

20 YEARS AGO

A beautiful night hangs over a typical suburban house in a typical suburban neighborhood. The yard is well kept, while manicured shrubbery decorates the property. Several windows are lit, and a grunting sound might be heard by any ear that might bother to press itself against a pane.

Crickets chirp in a steady, tranquil pulse. A wan moon glows through wisps of clouds.

And just as the beautiful night hangs over the house, a magnificent set of tits hangs over the ga-ga-eyed face of one Derrick Brooks, a bearded shuck-and-jive redneck who works "construction." Construction jobs pay well but not when you only work three days a year. Most of his time, therefore, is spent drinking beer, masturbating to porn, and living off the owner of those magnificent tits. Those tits, by the way, belong to a stunning and very capable thirtyish woman named April Russo. April is a nurse who rakes in good money, and, for whatever incomprehensible reason, is sharing her life—and her paycheck—with Derrick, and renting the house with no contribution from him. April hates the idea of being alone—hence, the nincompoop useless boyfriend who hangs like a mill-wheel around her neck and pisses all over the toilet seat. What is *wrong* with women?

But now, is it possible she's starting to get sick of him?

She's just finished trying, and failing, to engage in some satisfactory intercourse with Derrick. His action hadn't lasted—

"Really, Derrick? Thirty seconds?"

Derrick lay back beneath the momentous breasts. "Shit, girl, don't 'zaggerate. 'Twas more like forty or fifty."

Then he laughs and reaches for a beer. April pulls her nightgown around her, mutters, "Fuck," and stalks toward the stairs.

"Where you goin', lollipop?" Derrick inquires. "Don't you wanna cuddle none? See, all's it'll take is a little cuddlin', then I'se can get it right back up fer ya."

"FUCK YOU!" The very pissed off April delivers her answer and stomps up the stairs. "Only thing I wanna cuddle is a fuckin' zucchini! I'm gonna go take a shower!"

April's hot-as-hell legs flex as she mounts the stairs. Her ire and dissatisfaction percolate within her like living things.

"Why do I waste my time with that useless unemployed waste product?" she asks herself aloud.

When she barges into the bathroom and drops

her gown, those superior boobs seem to glow in the mirror, and her delectable hairless pubis sticks out like a fresh sourdough roll with a cut in it. The image of herself in the mirror is so positive it makes her forget just how insufferably pissed off she is at Derrick, but it only lasts a few moments before all that rancor pours back into her spirit, for now she could feel that insignificant spurtle of semen lolling around inside her disgruntled vagina. *MotherFUCKer!* she thinks. *Puts that puny mess in me and doesn't even last long enough for me to cum!*

Steaming in rage, April turns on the shower, but just as she steps in, she grimaces at a sudden very painful headache ...

Back downstairs, Derrick is watching porn. It's an oldie but goodie entitled *Anal Intruder*, starring the infamous Peter North. Pete hauls his hog out of the backside of a pretty but stupefied young actress named Sylvia Ryder, spins her around, and nuts all over her chest. What looks like over a dozen foot-long strings of spaghetti shoot out of his dick, leaving poor Miss Ryder shimmering in an appalled shock.

"Damn, that fella there can *shoot* a load, he can!" Derrick gives voice to his appreciation. "Sure as shit wish I could hose April down like that."

For any who might be interested, this was the first porn flick of Miss Ryder's career, and the last. A word of advice: if you're revolted by sperm, *don't* do porn.

Derrick watches the scene's final moments, grinning and rubbing his crotch. But suddenly, he jerks upright, feeling inexplicably ill, and then he clamps his hands against his temples at the instantaneous throb of a headache.

"Damn! Where'd this come from?"

He notices, too, a sudden low-pitched and rather eerie tone oscillating in his ears. The fury of the headache doubles. He winces.

"What the hell's that noise?"

And after that?

A scream rockets down from upstairs, a *woman's* scream.

"April!" he shouts.

He jumps up, cave-manning his way through the headache's staggering pain, and runs upstairs.

"April! I'm a-comin', baby!"

That weird tone still seems to be humming in the distance. Derrick bangs into the bathroom. Stops. Stares.

Some vague traces of purple light seem to mist the peripheries of his vision, which he doesn't understand. The shower water is still running. On the floor there seems to be some unpleasant flesh-colored glop, like pudding.

But April isn't there. In fact, she's not anywhere in the house.

She will never be heard from again …

THE PRESENT DAY

A bright blue summer sky hangs over the same typical suburban house. Only, now, many years later, the paint is flaking and faded, and the once well-maintained yard is an overgrown, straggly mess of mostly dead grass. To flagrantly steal from the important late-Victorian writer E.F. Benson, "weeds half-choked the front path, and the flower beds were a congestion of mingled wild and cultivated vegetations." A lopsided realtor sign stands in the front yard, apprising any onlooker that the property is available for sale or rent, but some upstanding neighbor has spray-painted on it: DON'T RENT, DON'T BUY, DON'T GO IN.

A car stops in front of the house, a small red Ford. Three women get out. First, there's Roxy, a buxom brunette, then Amy, a buxom scruffy blonde, then Larsa, buxom too but with long ink-black hair. All frowning slightly, they pull out suitcases. It's very hot out, so it might be appropriate to mention that little jewels of perspiration glitter in their cleavages.

Then another person alights from the vehicle, one who has a more focused interest in cleavage. This would be the car's driver, and his name is Ryan. He's very tall, slim, and dashingly handsome, but with a tint of perv about his expression.

Why so?

Because he *is* a perv, and damn proud of it. But that's beside the point.

The entire troupe seems to be in their mid-twenties. They all look up at the house …

Larsa stares blank-faced at the edifice. "This is it? That's the Marsten House? Looks like a typical house to me."

"Typical, huh?" Ryan contravenes. "At least eight women have disappeared in that house since the seventies."

Roxy's attention, usually dulled by an influx of pot gummies, perks up. "Any murders?"

"No."

"Well, that's a relief!" Amy says.

Ryan half-smiles. "But the eight boyfriends or husbands all died from heart attacks or strokes. Word is, they died of *fright*."

Roxy glares at him. "And we're spending the night here *why?*"

"I told you," Ryan says, looking not at Roxy's face but her massive breasts. "To prove the existence of the supernatural. I'll put it on my YouTube channel, and I'll get—I mean, *we'll* get rich."

"Sounds like bullshit to me," says Amy.

"Shut up, Amy," counters Larsa. "You got nothing better to do except sit around and wish you had a boyfriend."

Amy doesn't take kindly to the remark. "Fuck off, ho-bag. And don't tell me to shut up or I'll fold you in half, break your back, and make you tongue your own pussy."

Larsa chuckles. "Go ahead and try, ass-crack-face."

The two unsophisticated women converge, but just before fists would fly, Ryan breaks them up. "Cut that shit out! We got a lot of work to do, so let's go!"

"What? We're gonna break in?" Amy asks.

Now Ryan is looking at Amy's bosom instead of her face. "Noooo. A friend of mine works for the bank that repossessed the house." He holds up a key. "I slipped him some money and—presto!"

Roxy's ever-present frown sharpens. "I hope you slipped him more money than the twenty fuckin' bucks you're paying us."

"Don't make me laugh," Larsa intrudes. "Ryan's tighter than a bull's ass in fly season."

"You'll make plenty of money on the backend," Ryan assures with the conviction of any Hollywood producer, "so quit complaining."

But Amy needs to be assured of something else. "And you're feeding us too, right? I'm not investigating a haunted house on an empty stomach."

Larsa guffaws. "Amy, you've never done *anything* on an empty stomach!"

"Yeah? How about if I empty my stomach down the front of your whory shorts?"

Ryan is getting miffed. "Spare us the visuals, Amy, and yes, I'll order us Chinese. Now, come on, let's get started!"

It's nearly in a dramatic fashion that the four of them approach the house, suitcases in tow.

Ryan inserts his key and opens the front door. "Ladies first."

Roxy starts to enter.

"He said, ladies, Roxy. Not fuck-pigs," Larsa pipes up.

Roxy shakes her head. "One more word out of you and I'll pop your implants and squirt saline all over the place."

"Yeah?" Larsa challenges. "And one more word out of *you* and I'll pop your skull, and squirt—wait a minute! Nothing! 'Cos there's nothing *in* your skull!"

"Shut up and get in the house!" Ryan snaps. "Let's get this stuff unpacked!"

They enter the house, unimpressed.

Some sort of purplish electrical discharge hisses like a snake and dissipates. Unbeknownst to Ryan and his crew, a curtain in an upstairs window slowly opens, then shuts on its own.

In the living room, Roxy, Amy, Larsa, and Ryan start unpacking the suitcases, removing camera equipment, setting up tripods, and the like. From the last suitcase, Amy removes 6-packs of beer, the high-class stuff: Milwaukee's Best.

Next, Ryan passes out cameras. "B-Roll time, girls."

"What?" Roxy asks in her usual noncompliant tone of voice.

Ryan sighs. "Everybody turn your cameras on and walk around the house. It's called B-Roll. Incidental footage that can be edited in later."

Amy asks, "Why B-Roll? Why not C-Roll or D-Roll?"

"Or in your case, Amy, A-Roll because of what it rhymes with." Larsa smirks.

"I'll give you a flip-flop douche if you don't shut your cock-hole," Amy threatens.

"You girls gotta cut this shit out!" Ryan yells,

already sick of the animosity between them. "So let's get on with it. But first, like we talked about last night, I need you all to strip naked."

"The fuck?" Larsa says, wincing.

"Serious. It'll sell more copies of the DVD in the bonus features. Like we talked about."

"Fuck off, you pervert!" Amy snipes. "We never talked about any such thing!"

Ryan plays dumb. "We didn't? Oh, sorry, I thought we did. Anyway, we need all three of you to get nude. We'll get more hits, more money. What's the big deal? You walk around in your homes naked all the time. Walk around naked *here.*"

"No fuckin' way, Ryan," Roxy complains. "We're not giving you beat-off fodder, bitch."

Ryan sighs. "Okay, I'll pay you each an extra ten bucks. How's that?"

Roxy, Larsa, and Amy look at each other, shrug, then take off all their clothes.

What a fuckin' meat market! Ryan thinks, and yes, this will make for very usable beat-off fodder. He passes each girl a ten-dollar bill.

"That's more like it," Roxy says. "You're not gonna make suckers out of *us.*"

Now each naked girl, armed with a handicam, begins her slow trek about the home's rundown interior. Ryan wisely follows them with his more elaborate camera: wisely, because this position gives him an excellent opportunity to film their naked bodies from behind without their knowledge. He manages some superior shots of all three of their bare asses, not to mention pristine side-tit shots. Then he craftily lowers the camera and angles it upward to establish some stunning footage of Roxy's "baby-maker," like a clandestine upskirt shot, but the best part is she's wearing no skirt. Ryan's dick hardens at once. *I need to jerk off,* he thinks. *Bad …*

Amy asks, "What rooms have the most paranormal activity?"

"Not rooms. Room," Ryan answers. "The upstairs bathroom. That's the hot spot."

Larsa's brow goes up. "Why?"

"Because that's where all eight women reportedly vanished and were never seen again." Ryan reaches forward and turns the knob to the sinister bathroom. "Let's check it out …"

They enter the bathroom. Roxy, Amy, and Larsa trade ominous looks.

"Looks like an ordinary bathroom to me," Roxy insists.

Larsa's bare tits stick out like monuments of flesh. "It's creepy, though, just knowing eight women disappeared here. Let's go back downstairs."

"Yeah, Ryan. Time to order that Chinese food," Amy says, her tits, too, sticking out like the Venus de Milo.

Roxy turns, to add to the potency of the image. *Fuck!* Ryan thinks, barely able to contain himself. *It's a Tit-Stravaganza!*

"And you can tell us everything you know about this fucked-up house," Roxy urges.

Not long afterward, the B-Roll mission

accomplished, the four of them are sitting at the kitchen table, eating Chinese food out of cartons.

"—and his name was Septimus Marsten," Ryan continues his disquisition, trying hard not to deliberately eyeball the three pairs of nude breasts sitting before him. "He bought this house new in 1950."

Amy is stuffing her face with roast pork fried rice. "Let me guess, he was a serial killer."

"No," Ryan negates. "He was a physics professor at the college. So was his wife, Asenath. But they didn't just work for the college; they also worked for the government."

Larsa wolfs down some beef chow mein. "Doing what, exactly?"

Ryan grins ominously. "No one knows for sure. But it was something to do with physics, quantum mechanics, shit like that. They did lots of research for the government and made lots of money."

Roxy crunches a piece of shrimp toast. "I'm not seeing evidence of a lot of money in this shitty house."

"Maybe not," Ryan comes back, "but a woman at the bank said Marsten had a million bucks in his account. The day before he died, he withdrew it all in cash."

"So what happened to all that money?" Amy asks.

Ryan goes on with his tale. "Marsten had a heart attack while eating McDonald's at this very table. The police concluded that his wife, Asenath, ran off with the money. But that's not what really happened. Asenath disappeared without a trace too. The rumor is she hid the money somewhere in the house first."

Roxy about hacks up a piece of shrimp toast. "Fuck that shit, man! If there's a million bucks in this dump, we're taking it!"

Ryan smiles. "That's the idea. It'll be two birds with one stone. First, we shoot our paranormal investigation and make a fuck ton on YouTube. Then we find the hidden million—we'll be rolling in dough for a long time!"

Roxy switches to sweet and sour chicken, eating it with her fingers. "Oh, really. And how are we just gonna *find* the million bucks?"

Now Ryan's grin is absolutely surreptitious. "Leave that to the *brains* of this operation. I got a plan."

Larsa can't resist. "It's a good thing Amy's not the brains of this operation, 'cos she's got *dick* for brains."

Amy grimaces at Larsa and holds up an egg roll. "Keep running your trap, bitch, and I'll ruin this perfectly good eggroll by stuffing it up your snatch."

"Stuff it up your own snatch, cuntster. It'll be the best action you've had in years."

"Fuck you! I get laid all the time!" Amy yells.

"By whose dog?"

"Eat my shit!" Amy counters. "When I was in first grade, I was voted Prettiest Girl In Class!"

Roxy makes a disapproving face. "I've seen rectal warts prettier than you—"

Ryan winces. "Damn! I thought you girls were best friends!"

"We are," Roxy says. "We just razz each other sometimes. Amy could get laid anytime time she wanted … if she cleared all those cob webs out of her pussy."

Larsa has to add, "Yeah, and if she doesn't get a dick in her soon, her twat will heal shut."

Amy's face pinkens and she bursts out in tears. "Ryan! Make them stop picking on me!"

"Now look what you've done!" Ryan exclaims. "You don't need to be mean to her. Try to get along! You should apologize!"

Larsa pats Amy on the shoulder. "I'm sorry, sweetie. I was just kidding. Come on, let's kiss and make up." She leans forward, making a Kissy Face.

Amy glares. "If you try to kiss me, I'll throw up in your mouth!"

"Yeah?" Larsa retorts. "How about if I stand you on your head, scissor you, and shit down your pussy?"

"Stop it, both of you!" Ryan barks. "You two are gonna fuck this shoot up! We gotta get to work!"

Later, they're all in the shabby living room. Ryan picks up one of the suitcases. "You girls just hang out here a while and have a few beers. I'm going upstairs to tweak the script on my laptop. Then we'll officially start the shoot tonight."

Roxy, Amy, and Larsa all smile.

Amy says, "It's beer o'clock!"

"Sounds good to me!" Roxy adds.

Larsa gets three beers and passes them out. "Bar's open!"

At this point, Ryan departs to the upstairs, lugging a suitcase. He goes into one bedroom but stops, noticing a framed picture on the dresser. The picture shows a studious older man with a goatee, arm-in-arm with a sultry big-boobed blonde in her 40s. Ryan turns the picture over and reads:

"'Septimus and Asenath Marsten, 1955.' Well, looks like Asenath wasn't lacking in the Rack Department." He shrugs, puts the picture back, and opens the suitcase. He sets up his laptop on the desk, then pulls out a bag of mini cameras. He grins sleazily. "It's about time I got an eyeful of these road hogs ..."

Now Ryan commences to sneaking around from bedroom to bedroom, planting the tiny cameras. Then he sneaks down to the downstairs bathroom and starts planting one in the shower.

But does he happen to notice the man-sized scary shadow-shape that rises behind him?

No!

The perfect face of mischief, Ryan finishes adjusting the settings on the little camera, then rubs his hands together in lewd satisfaction. "And now for a very special episode of Cooze TV!"

Ryan leaves the room, but that large shadow-shape is still shifting around there. Then it disappears with a crackly electric discharge as a fast hollow laugh resounds and fades away.

Roxy, Amy, and Larsa are sitting on the couch in the living room, drinking beer.

Roxy burps. "Damn, I'm hornier than a jackal

full of Spanish fly."

"I could go for a cock in me too," Amy points out, "balls deep."

"Well, there's always Ryan," Larsa suggests.

Amy spits out a mouthful of beer. "Ryan? I wouldn't fuck him with an orangutan's pussy."

Roxy contemplates this and shrugs her shoulders. "I would ... I guess."

"Ewww!" Amy and Larsa squeal.

Roxy gives the insinuation a moment's further thought and thinks, *Yeah, I guess they're right.* Her scowl out the front window changes her mind. "Fuck. It's getting dark. Makes this place even creepier, especially knowing what happened here. Eight guys drop dead from fright, and eight girls disappear."

"And if there really is a million bucks in this house, how are we gonna find it?" Amy asks.

"Ryan said he's got a plan," Larsa reminds them. "Let's give him the benefit of the doubt and see what happens."

"Can't hurt, I guess. He may be a pervert and a scrounge, but he seems pretty smart ..."

Ryan strides into the room. He grabs a beer and opens it. "Okay, girls. The shooting script's tweaked. Why don't you all go upstairs and pick a bedroom, get some sleep? We won't be starting till late."

"How late?" Roxy asks.

Ryan smiles sinisterly. "3:15, the Witching Hour. You know, like Amityville?"

Larsa frowns. "Whatever. But I *could* go for a nap right now."

Amy yawns and stretches her arms, the action of which grandly elucidates her bare breasts. "Me too. I need some shut-eye."

"I'm gonna take a shower first," Roxy says.

Ryan looks sternly at her. "Fine, but make sure you use the downstairs shower. That goes for all of you."

Roxy's big bare tits stand out like sentinels. "Upstairs, downstairs, what difference does it make?"

"It makes plenty of difference," Ryan goes on. "Every single woman who disappeared in this house, including Asenath Marsten, disappeared in the *upstairs* bathroom."

Roxy gulps. "Got'cha. Shit, I *can't* disappear. I have to see my parole officer tomorrow. What about you? What are you gonna do?"

"I'll start putting up the camera lights," Ryan replies, "and maybe—"

"And maybe jerk off?" Larsa finishes for him.

Ryan smirks as if the suggestion is preposterous. "Are you kidding me? I've got so many chicks following me down the street, I don't *need* to jerk off. I'm up to my *neck* in pussy."

Amy and Larsa start out of the room, laughing.

"Sure you are, Romeo," Larsa says.

Roxy heads toward the downstairs hall. "Oh, and Ryan? I'll kick your dick in and squash your balls if I catch you trying to peek in on me in the shower."

Ryan smiles. "I wouldn't dream of it ..."

Upstairs, Amy and Larsa each choose bedrooms for themselves. Roxy slips into the downstairs bathroom. But during these traversions, Ryan has already established himself in his own room, in front of his laptop. He's masturbating like a man with a mission, huffing and puffing, his face ludicrously contorted.

Just now, he's looking at Roxy taking a shower, suds sliding down those immense and immaculate mounds of gleaming flesh, each big dark nipple decorating the breast like an angel atop a resplendent Christmas tree. Ryan's cheeks billow and his eyes cross, as he jerks onward until …

"Aw, shit! Here it comes! The motherlode!"

And the "motherlode" it is, multiple spurts multiple feet long, all over him.

"How do you like them cookies, bitch?" he asks Roxy's oblivious image on the computer screen.

But no sooner has he mopped up the pearlescent mess with a Brawny paper towel, does he click the necessary buttons on his keyboard in order to change cameras.

"Let's see what these other tit-wagons are doing …"

On the next screen, Amy is asleep on her bed. She's on her belly, and her butt's sticking up.

"Looks like she's asking to get her temperature taken," Ryan observes. "Well, the doctor is *in!*"

Oh, blessed youth! Ryan's erection, even after the voluminous orgasm, has not slackened one iota, and he immediately wastes no time in recommencing some serious masturbation. All the while, his pervert eyes fix wide on the screen and, sequently, Amy's magnificent ass. Less than a minute later, more sperm fires out of Ryan's dickhole.

"Wow!"

But should he try for another?

He would indeed try for another …

He switches to the next camera, where Larsa sleeps with one big beautiful bare boob out.

"Watch me turn this dizzy dunce into a rumbun," Ryan promises himself, and there he goes again, beating his meat like the Zombie Apocalypse is just outside his door. Staring intently at Larsa's tit, his cock once again answers the summons of his hand.

And—

"Fuck yeah!" comes his gleeful grunt as still more sperm manage to make an exodus from his erection. "A Three-Fer! Haven't done that since junior high!"

Twilight pulls its obsidian caul across the sky as the Marsten House settles down for another endless night. The house seems to sit one half in the real world and the other half in some sinister *other* … A wan sickle moon hangs low. Crickets chirrup in a dark, throbbing dirge.

Inside the house, a clock is ticking. It reads 2:45 a.m.

Ryan barges into Larsa's bedroom with much ado. Larsa remains asleep with one spectacular boob out.

"Rise and shine, cutie!" Ryan yells.

"Ug. Fuck." Larsa opens her eyes, grimacing, and pulls her boob back in. "Eat dog shit and die!"

"How congenial!" Ryan replies. In truth, his dick is still half hard. "Come on, get up and come downstairs! We're starting soon."

Larsa makes a retching sound at this information.

Next, Ryan barges into Roxy's room. She's asleep spread-eagled on the bed, serious camel toe showing through her panties, and this vision does little to diminish Ryan's partial boner.

"Foxy Roxy!" he yells as loudly as possible. "Get your ass up and meet us downstairs!"

Roxy's eyes blink open; then she's furious. "Go to hell and blow the devil, you skinny fuck!"

"Charming as ever! The kind of girl every guy wants to take home to meet Mom."

"Cram it!" Roxy moans and buries her head in the pillow as Ryan leaves.

Neither of them notice the giant shadow-shape manifested against the wall with arms outstretched.

Ryan's next barge is into Amy's room. Amy is sidled over in the covers, snoring.

"Up and at 'em, cupcake!" he trumpets. "It's time to start the shoot!"

Amy awakens with a fierce frown, then sits up, looking appalled. "Damn you, you dick-shit! I was dreaming that George Clooney was corn-holing me, and you woke me up before I could cum!"

"My apologies, my dear, and my apologies to George as well. Ass out of bed. Downstairs. Now!"

Ryan exits quickly. Amy gets up and follows him.

She exits just as the shadow-shape appears. The

entity seems frustrated, slapping arms down in anger before disappearing again.

Now we find our team in the living room, the women gloriously naked. They're standing around Ryan as he addresses them.

"The hour is at hand, girls," he announces overdramatically. "It's time for us to solve the mystery of the Marsten House and find that million bucks."

"Great," Roxy says, less than enthusiastically. "So what's this plan of yours?"

Larsa scratches her armpit. "Yeah, since you *are* the brains of the operation, let's hear it."

Ryan smiles knowingly. "Simple. We're gonna find out where the money is by utilizing a tried-and-true method. We're going to *ask the house* itself!"

Roxy does not look impressed. "Really, fuck-nub? You're going to ask *the house?*"

Amy smolders. "Of all the stupid fuckleberry shit! How can you ask the house anything?"

"Simple, Amy. With a good old fashioned Ouija board."

Larsa frowns. "I looked in all those suitcases, and there was no fuckin' Ouija board in any of them."

Ryan smiles confidentially, nodding. "I'm glad you mentioned that. Because, you see, there *is* a Ouija board."

"No there *isn't!* What the *fuck* are you talking about?"

Five minutes later, Larsa is very much finding out what Ryan is talking about because she's stretched out naked on the floor, and, with stick-on black letters, Ryan has made a Ouija board on her bare belly. The room is darker now, lit only by flickering candles.

"See? A *human* Ouija board!" Ryan celebrates.

Larsa smirks, looking down at the letters on her belly. There's also a row of black numbers and the words HELLO and GOODBYE.

"This is the dick-stupidest thing I ever heard of!" she says.

"Don't be a naysayer," Ryan advises. "There's all kinds of documentation that most spirits are horny because they get no sex in the afterlife. So they'll be much more inclined to respond if the Ouija board is a hot chick instead of a plastic thing that says Hasbro on it. It's all about positive erotic imagery. It's like a magnet for spirits."

"He's right, Larsa," Amy concurs. "I think I read something about that once."

Larsa scowls. "You haven't read *dick*, Amy, so don't talk shit! You can't read a stop sign!"

"Fuck you!"

Roxy shrugs. "But it kind of makes sense when you look at it that way. Spirits would probably take more notice of a pretty girl with no clothes on."

"You're absolutely right," Ryan says. "I've read tons of studies by parapsychologists that support the idea. Put a naked girl in the room, and horny spirits will come calling. To see what they can't see in the netherworld. Like driving a meat truck past a pack of pit bulls."

"It's dick-stupid cockamamie bullshit!" Larsa complains. "So you're gonna ask the house questions and its gonna answer on my fucking *stomach*?"

"Precisely," Ryan answers.

Amy looks puzzled. "But don't you need a whatchimacallit? A planchette?"

"Anything can work as a planchette," Ryan says. "Even this." He picks a beer cap off the floor, puts it top-side down on Larsa's stomach, then uses his fingertip to show how easily it slides around. "There. See?"

But Larsa is still scowling in displeasure. "Well, get on with it, then! I feel asinine like this!"

"That's because you *are* asinine, Larsa," Amy comments. "You *are* asinine—"

"Fuck off, you food-card nitwit!" Larsa comes back. "I'll arm-fuck you and pop your eyeballs out from the *inside!*"

"Suck my gash!" Amy counters.

"No way," Larsa says. "I'm allergic to yeast—"

"Stop it!" Ryan yells. "Jeez, you girls are like animals!"

"*I'm* not like an animal," Roxy says. "I'm ladylike and genteel—"

Larsa blurts a laugh. "Gimme a break, Roxy! How many guys did you bang at Dick Troggler's New Year's Eve Party last year? Ten? Fifteen? You bragged about it on your fucking Facebook, for dick's sake!"

Roxy's expression crumbles. "Oh, big deal. I was drunk."

"Everybody just SHUT THE FUCK UP so we can do this!" Ryan bellows.

The room goes quiet. Candlelight flickers on walls. Ryan gives Roxy a pad and a pen. "I'm gonna ask questions, and you're gonna write down any responses, okay?"

"Sure," Roxy says. "Wow, this might be fun!"

"That's the spirit!" Ryan approves. "Amy, you kneel down beside Larsa on her right side, and I'll kneel down at her left." Once situated, Ryan hands Amy a blindfold. "And we'll put these on so we can't see the board; otherwise our subconscious minds might force the planchette to specific letters. Are you ready, Larsa?"

"Blow me," Larsa replies. "This is ridiculous."

Ryan rolls his eyes. "Fine. Amy, Roxy? Are you ready?"

Amy and Roxy both nod.

"Roxy, turn on the camera now."

Roxy goes to a camera that's already been set up on a tripod and is pointing down at Larsa.

Ryan continues with his all-important instructions. "Amy, put one fingertip on the bottle cap, then pull down your blindfold."

Amy does this.

Ryan does too, then takes a deep breath and says, "Okay, here we go …"

A long eerie pause hangs over the group. Orange candlelight flickers over their faces.

Ryan begins: "Hello. Are there any spirits, ghosts, or phantoms here?"

The bottle cap goes to NO.

"It said no!" Roxy exclaims.

Ryan looks flustered. "What are you then?"

The bottle cap quickly slides back and forth to lots of letters on Larsa's belly.

She squirms. "That fucking *tickles*!"

"Hold still!" Ryan demands. "What did it spell, Roxy?"

Roxy is shaking, eyes wide on her pad. "It said, 'I am a specter composed of revenant electromagnetic energy.'"

Ryan looks alarmed but excited. "Holy shit! That's a pretty scientific answer!" He refocuses. "To the spirit who just answered, is your name Septimus Marsten?

The bottle cap goes to YES.

"Yes!" Roxy squeals.

Ryan takes a deep breath. "Professor Marsten, where is your wife, Asenath?"

The bottlecap zooms back and forth over letters. Again, Larsa wriggles.

Roxy recites back, "'That big-tit fucksicle? When we worked together at the physics lab, she fucked every guy in the place, the dirty whore. And she only married me for my money. I should've buried the bitch in the backyard.'"

"Oh, dear," Ryan mutters. "Professor, eight women, including your wife, disappeared in this house. Why did they disappear?"

The bottlecap jerks back and forth again.

Roxy: "'Because of my genius,' it said."

"Where did they disappear to?" Ryan asks next.

The bottlecap moves around, and Roxy recites, "He said, 'Into the house.'"

Ryan pauses, scratches his head, then asks,

"Professor, where is the money?"

This time, the bottlecap jerks back and forth for quite a while. Larsa grits her teeth, trying not to move, while Roxy scribbles frantically in her pad.

"Fuck!" Roxy exclaims. "He said 'My drunk slut of a wife stole it and hid it in the house, then she put digitalis in my milkshake and killed me, the treacherous tramp!'"

Ryan looks amazed. "Damn! So Professor Marsten was really murdered! And by his wife! Professor, do you mean that the money is in this house?"

Yet again, the bottlecap jerks back and forth.

"'Not the house you're in,'" Roxy says. "'The *other* house.'"

Ryan squints, confused. "What other house, Professor?"

The bottlecap moves some more. Roxy squeals again, looking at her pad. "Oh my God! He said 'Fuck! I gotta go! The evil bitch is coming!'"

"Who is coming, Professor?" Ryan pleads. "Your wife?"

Several moments go by; the bottlecap doesn't budge. Jittering, Ryan and Amy push their blindfolds up.

"How do you like that?" Ryan remarks. "Asenath murdered the professor! What a revelation!"

"Yeah," Amy says, "but where did she hide the money? What about this other house? Did Marsten own two?"

"I don't know ..." Ryan answers, flustered.

Larsa, exasperated, cranes her neck up. "We're done now, right? The foolishness is over?"

But Amy's eyes shoot wide open and she points to Larsa's belly. "It's not over yet! Look!"

The bottlecap has moved by itself to the word HELLO.

"Shit!" Ryan yells. "Let's get back to it!"

He and Amy pull their blindfolds back on and each put a finger on the bottlecap.

Ryan asks, "Is this Asenath Marsten?"

The bottlecap shoots to YES.

"Yes!" Roxy trumpets.

Ryan now jitters with excitement. "Asenath, where is your husband?"

The bottlecap jerks back and forth, and Roxy recites, "She said, 'I sent the old fuck packing. He's a tightwad no-dick piece of garbage. He had all that cash and wouldn't even buy me a new car!'"

Ryan is insistent, "Asenath? Where did you hide the money?"

The bottlecap continues moving over Larsa's stomach.

Roxy says, "'That skin-flint horse's ass couldn't even fuck me. Last time he got hard was when Truman was in office!'"

Ryan's getting flustered. "Asenath? Where is the money?"

The bottlecap zooms around. Roxy's expression is suddenly excited. "She said, 'Do you want me to give you a hint?'"

Ryan frantically answers, " Yes! Yes, please. Asenath! Give us a hint!"

Once again, the bottlecap goes into action, but Roxy looks puzzled. "Asenath just said, 'What brings May flowers?'"

Ryan raises his blindfold, energized.

Amy frowns. "That old kid's rhyme—"

"April showers bring May flowers!" Roxy blurts.

Ryan makes a knowing nod. "Yep. April showers. The last girl to disappear in this house was named *April* Russo, and her dying boyfriend said she was in the *shower* when she disappeared!" He goes to address the board on Larsa's stomach again but says disappointedly, "Shit. Look."

They all look at Larsa's stomach. The bottlecap has moved to the word GOODBYE.

"So I'm done now, right?" Larsa assumes.

"Yeah. It looks like the Ouija show is over. Let's go upstairs and take a *very close look* at the upstairs shower."

Larsa sits up, trying to peel the black letters from her stomach but having no luck. "What the fuck? Ryan, these stupid-ass things won't come off. What did you stick 'em on with?"

"Just regular Elmer's." He pulls a glue tube out of his pocket and gives it to Larsa.

She fumes, "You asshole! This is *Crazy Glue!*"

Ryan scratches his head. "Oops, my bad. But it'll probably wear off ..."

Larsa's face turns red. "You fucking moron! Now I've got fucking Ouija board shit stuck to me!"

This, Ryan disregards with a smirk. "Quit bellyaching, Larsa. We've got important shit to do here and you're whining about your stomach. Everybody! The upstairs bathroom!"

As Amy, Roxy, and Larsa all begin clambering upstairs, Ryan stays momentarily behind, retrieving the camera. Suddenly, Larsa goes bug-eyed and enraged. "Damn you, Ryan! Get your hand off my ass, or so help me I'll cut it off!"

But when she turns, it's to see Ryan still at the bottom of the stairs, looking up. "What?"

Larsa is flabbergasted. "For fuck's sake! I just felt a hand squeezing my ass! I thought it was you!"

"Wish it was," Ryan says, grinning. "But it wasn't; I'm down here—"

Just then, Amy shouts, "OWWW! Something pinched my nipple, and I mean *hard!*"

And next? There's a loud, fat *FWAP!* and Roxy falls down, hands to crotch.

"Fuck! What just kicked me in the cunt?"

Amy helps her up. As they all hurry for the top of the stairs, Larsa HOWLS in pain. The Ouija letters are being ripped from her body as if by some invisible agency, stretching her skin as each is yanked off. Larsa clutches her abdomen and sinks to the stairs.

Ryan considers the scene reflectively. "Hmmm. This is getting more interesting by the minute. Assaults by phantasmal entities, no doubt connected to the women who disappeared here."

"You mean their ghosts?" Amy conjectures.

"For lack of a better word, yes."

"Fuck this shit, man!" Larsa bellows. "Let's get out of here!"

"Yeah!" Roxy agrees. "I just got kicked in the fur-burger!"

Ryan looks at them scoldingly. "Girls. We may

be on the brink of finding a million dollars. You sure you want to leave now?"

The naked trio all kind of shuffle in place together on the stairs.

"You're right. Fuck it," Roxy says. "We'll stay."

"Thought so," Ryan declares. "Onward now, to the bathroom!"

They go the rest of the way up, then down the hall, then enter the bathroom. Their faces turn inquisitively toward the shower.

"Like I said the first time," Roxy repeats. "It looks like an ordinary bathroom."

"Yeah, but looks are deceiving," Ryan remarks.

Larsa stiffens in place, alarmed. "Listen! Do you hear that?"

A sourceless *scratching* sound gradually becomes heard by them all.

"Yeah," Roxy says.

"Indeed," Ryan adds, "and scratching sounds are frequently linked to the proximity of demonic forces."

"Demons?" Larsa echoes. "You never said anything about demons!"

Roxy glares. "Yeah! This is just supposed to be a dumb-ass YouTube investigation!"

But the scratching sound eerily continues.

Larsa points at Amy. "It's not demons! Look! It's just Amy, scratching her hairy pussy!"

Amy, scratching her crotch, glances up, none the wiser. "Huh?"

Ryan is irked. "Come on, girls; this is serious. Act like you give a shit. Look around, see if you can find anything out of order."

They poke around the bathroom a moment, then Roxy indicates the mirror. "There!"

On the glass, in barely visible finger streaks, is the word ATTIC.

"Looks like *somebody's* talking to us," Roxy says.

"Okay," Ryan announces. "Let's go!"

They file out of the bathroom.

Once it's empty, a faint luminous outline appears superimposed on the mirror: the face of an attractive but cunning-looking woman.

It's the face of the woman Ryan previously noticed in the photograph, that of Asenath Marsten ... Tiny blue threads of electrical sparks seem to crackle around her face.

In the hall, Ryan pulls down the spring-loaded attic stairs. "Which one of you brave beauties wants to go first?"

Frowning, Amy, Roxy, and Larsa all give Ryan the finger.

"You're the man," Larsa snipes, "so be one for a change. Get *your* ass up there."

Ryan sighs, looks discomfited, then mounts the pull-down stairs and goes into the attic. He clicks on a light.

"Well?" Larsa asks. "Anything?"

Ryan's voice booms down excitedly. "Damn straight! A shitload of scientific instruments, and they're all turned on ..."

But then he goes silent.

Amy peers upward. "Ryan? You all right?"

Ryan does not answer.

"Hey! Ass-crack-face!" Larsa yells. "What's going on up there?"

No answer. The girls start to look worried.

Roxy calls up, "Ryan! Wanna blow job? I'll even swallow!"

No answer.

"Something's really wrong," Larsa determines. "We're gonna have to go up. Come on, ghosts can't hurt us."

"Oh, really?" Amy retorts. "A ghost grabbed your butt, kicked Roxy in the pussy, and pinched my nipple!"

Larsa scowls. "Don't be a sissy!"

Reluctantly, then, they all climb up and into the attic.

"Oh, my God," Roxy mutters.

Ryan is unconscious on the floor with his pants down to his ankles. His flaccid penis is out … and a foot long. The girls all stare slack-jawed at it.

"You gotta be shitting me," Roxy murmurs.

Amy brings a hand to her mouth. "Yeah. I had no idea he was so hung."

"It looks like a damn baby's leg," Larsa mutters.

Roxy nudges Ryan with her foot. His big flaccid dick wobbles.

"Ryan! Wake up! Your dick's out, you idiot!" Roxy yells.

Amy grins and snaps a pic with her cellphone. "Here's one for the internet!"

Larsa bellows, "Ryan! Wake the fuck up!"

Ryan gradually regains consciousness, then, embarrassed, pulls his pants up. He's groggy.

"Fuck. Of all the shit …"

"What happened?" Roxy demands. "Why were your fucking pants down?"

Ryan's brow goes up. "You won't believe this, but I just got my ashes hauled by a ghost!"

"You're right," Roxy snaps. "I don't believe it—"

Ryan smiles as if in deep reminiscence. "Best lay of my life. And lemme tell ya. I've been laid a *lot*."

"That's great, Gene Simmons," Roxy says. "But where's all this scientific stuff you were talking about?"

Ryan points. "Over there."

The girls turn and see shelves full of scientific equipment: lights blinking, antennae twirling, oscilloscopes wavering.

Larsa stares. "What the fuck is all this shit?"

"The tools of Marsten's trade, I think," Ryan speculates.

Amy peers down at the floor. "All this stuff is directly above the *shower*."

Ryan nods grimly. "I'm starting to put two and two together," he muses as they climb back down.

Roxy's bare tits stick out in utter perfection. "Yeah?"

Ryan goes on, "Marsten and his wife were *physicists*. What if they were examining theories about alternate dimensions and parallel planes of existence?"

"Yeah!" Roxy agrees. "And all that equipment in the attic is the stuff they need to—"

"Right," Ryan says, "To create a portal, a *door*."

"You mean a door to another dimension?" Larsa asks. Her bare tits, as well, stand out in a demonstration of mammarian magnificence.

Ryan nods, arms crossed. "Yes, and that door must somehow be in the shower. That's where Asenath and those other girls disappeared, and they're probably still there: in a parallel dimension."

Roxy looks puzzled. "So *that's* where the money is?"

"I think so," Ryan says. "And there's only one way for us to get it …"

Suddenly, Larsa is slammed against the wall by an unseen force. Amid more *peeling* sounds, the remaining black glued-on Ouija letters are being torn off her stomach.

"Fuck! That hurts like a motherfucker!"

Ryan uselessly attempts to go to her aid. As he does, Amy shrieks, clasping her boob.

"Fuck!" she exclaims. She cossets it in her hand to show a vicious bitemark. Her nipple is dripping blood.

As Roxy moves closer to try and help, there is a fat *FWAP!* Roxy grunts, clutches her crotch, and falls to the floor.

"Another kick in the panty hamster?" Ryan asks.

Cringing, Roxy nods in pain. "Ten times harder than the last one! Felt like it popped my fuckin' uterus!"

Ryan's eyes widen, and he goes up on tiptoes. Blue staticky electrical discharge crackles over his crotch. He is in ecstasy. "Somebody's feeling up my junk! Damn, it feels so good!"

Roxy struggles back to her feet, while Larsa is still rubbing her belly, and Amy is holding her bitten boob.

"What a rip-off," Roxy sputters. "We get assaulted but you get fondled?"

Ryan doesn't look surprised. "Hey, I'm a pretty good-looking guy! The discorporated spirits in this house are *women*. Of course they're hot for me, but they're jealous of you. Happens all the time with chicks."

"Listen to the Ken Doll over here," Amy says.

"Oh, yeah," Roxy sneers. "Ryan's so hot, even the ghosts can't keep their hands off him."

Ryan cocks a brow and grins. "Your words, not mine."

Roxy glares. "Shut up, you butt-nut! What do we do now?"

Ryan takes a quarter out of his pocket. "Coin toss. Larsa, it's me and you. Call it." He flips the coin.

"Heads!" Larsa calls out.

"Tails, you lose. Amy, Roxy. Roxy, you call it." He flips it again.

Roxy's tits jump when she calls out, "Tails!"

Ryan shows tails. He smiles. "Amy, Larsa, sudden death time. Amy, call it."

He flips the coin yet again.

"Uh, fuck!" Amy says. "Heads!"

"Tails," he says. "Sorry, Amy. You lose."

Amy looks baffled. "Lose what? What does that mean?"

Ryan shrugs lackadaisically. "It means *you* go into the portal."

"Fuck that!" she cries, outraged. "Eat my shorts, bonehead!"

Ryan cannot resist. "You're not wearing shorts.

You're not wearing anything."

"Uh, well, I mean if I *was* wearing any, you could eat 'em. I ain't going into any damn *portal*!"

Roxy and Larsa scowl at her.

"Fair is fair," Larsa says.

Roxy nods. "Yeah, Amy. You lost the toss. So get your dumb ass into that bathroom and go to the other dimension."

"FUCK YOU!" Amy bellows.

Roxy grins. "If you don't, me and Larsa will beat your pussy like a pork schnitzel at the German restaurant …"

Amy sullenly resigns herself to the inevitable. Ryan urges her into the bathroom.

"Come on, Amy," he assures her. "It's no big deal. Just … go to the other dimension, find the money, bring it back, and we're all made in the shade."

"FUCK YOU!" Amy reiterates sulkily.

Larsa twists Amy's arm.

"Okay, okay!" Whining, she submits.

"I thought so, jizz-head," Larsa snickers.

Amy surveys the bathroom, upset, teary-eyed. "So where even is this portal? What do I do?"

Ryan replies while ogling Amy's bare breasts, despite the blood continuing to ooze from the bitten nipple. "I'd guess the shower itself somehow opens the portal. When April Russo disappeared, she was taking a *shower*." Then he pauses as if a great idea just popped into his head. "I'm a genius! Wait here a minute."

Ryan rushes downstairs, returning with Amy's cellphone in a plastic bag tied on a loop of a string.

He puts the string around her neck, the bagged camera lying on her mountainous tits.

"What the fuck?" Amy questions.

"Take it with you, and if you get over there, call me. You can give us a blow by blow. Who knows? Maybe it'll work."

Amy frowns. "Shit, this is scary. I don't think I can do it ..."

Roxy shoves Amy deeper into the bathroom. "You're going! So take a fuckin' shower!"

Amy is distraught, still teary-eyed. "What? In front of everybody?" As if she hasn't been bare-assed naked in front of them all day.

"Okay, we'll wait in the hall," Ryan says. He, Larsa, and Roxy leave the bathroom. Ryan closes the door. "We'll just have to wait and see what happens," he concludes

Roxy and Larsa lean against the wall, arms crossed, looking lascivious. Once they hear the water start running, Larsa winks at Roxy, then turns to Ryan.

"So, Ryan? What are you doing after this?"

"Counting out our money, I hope."

"No, no," Roxy corrects. "She means after all this haunted house shit is done."

"How should I know? We're doing important stuff today. I'm focusing on that."

Roxy can't believe it. "Wow, Ryan. You sure can be a dim bulb sometimes."

"Let me put it this way, Einstein," Larsa intervenes. "How about you fuck us like a couple of two-dollar whores?"

"Got your attention yet?" Roxy adds. "Ever

heard of a three-way?"

Ryan pauses, looking skeptical. "Any time I've tried to get in either of your pants, you've given me the bigtime bum's rush."

"Yeah," Larsa admits, "but that was before we knew you had a ten-pound pork loin in *your* pants."

"Don't be greedy," Roxy says. "You need to share that shit."

"Oh, so *now* you want me?" he says with a snide smile. "Well, sorry, girls, your time-held fantasy will have to wait. I'm busy."

Roxy and Larsa make incredulous faces. "You're turning down free pussy? You?" Larsa asks.

Roxy chimes in, "What real man turns away pussy? We'll bang your brains out on this floor right now!"

But now Ryan has a *playing hard to get* look. "Sorry, but there are things in this world more important than you getting boned, and one of them is this investigation. You ought to be ashamed of yourselves. Right now, Amy's in that shower, risking her life for us."

"She's a ditz and a douche nozzle!" Roxy exclaims.

Larsa nods, arms folded under her whopper breasts. "Yeah, and she sucks guys' wangs for McDonald's money."

But Ryan ignores this. "Speaking of which, we better check on her, make sure she's okay."

"Shit, she's probably pronging herself with the toilet-brush handle!" Larsa says, getting pissed.

"Or the toilet-brush head!" Roxy suggests.

Ryan knocks on the bathroom door. "Amy? How are things going in there?"

Amy's beautiful nude body is all sudsed up in the shower. Her hands glide around her superlative breasts, then slowly circle down to her pubis. They linger there. She seems to be contemplating masturbation, but she really can't focus due to the annoying sound of the water hitting the plastic bag and cellphone around her neck.

"Fuck it," she says to herself. "I can't cum like this …" Then she looks around inside the shower stall. "Well, portal or whatever you are. Here I am …"

Suddenly, Amy's eyes go wide with alarm as the shower stall fills with throbbing purple light and what seem to be shifting kaleidoscopic squares.

Her eyes bulge. She sees something, but when she opens her mouth to scream, nothing comes out. At once, she's stricken by wave after wave of uncontrollable jitters …

Back in the hallway, Ryan, Roxy, and Larsa are still waiting. Ryan knocks on the door again.

"Amy!" he yells.

No response is forthcoming. Ryan knocks louder.

"Amy!"

Larsa smirks. "She probably passed out from all that beer she chugged. No wonder AA kicked her out."

Amy is still shaking. The weird kaleidoscopic shapes throb brightly, and she is being pulled toward them … the flesh of her body stretching: breasts, belly, face … all of it is moving toward the light …

She can hear Ryan's stout knocks from the other side of the door. "Come on," he yells. "This is serious! We're going in!"

The door thunks and rattles. Just as it is about to break, Amy's flesh is ripped from her bones, and a second later, she is dragged into the throbbing portal of purple light …

Kicking the door in, Ryan and the girls barge inside.

"Amy!" he shouts. "Where are y—"

The shower is still running, but there's no sign of Amy. Remnants of a gooey flesh-colored plasm lay on the shower floor.

Roxy and Larsa stand speechless.

"Holy shit!" Ryan blurts. "She did it! She crossed over to the parallel dimension!"

They all gaze into the shower, dumbfounded.

Roxy dips her hand into the slop-like teleplasm. "Damn. I know she's a horny brain-dead ditz, but I hope this isn't all that's left of her …"

Ryan speculates. "Maybe there's some remnant energy left over from Amy's transference. Roxy, why don't you go in the shower right now and see if you can get through too?"

Roxy laughs. "Why don't you bend over real

hard and suck your own dick? You think I want to turn into slop?"

Ryan looks winsomely to Larsa. "Take one for the team?"

"Drink my diarrhea," Larsa eloquently replies.

Roxy leans against the wall, tapping her foot. "Well? You're the self-proclaimed the *brains* of this operation, Ryan. What's next?"

Ryan contemplates the question with some anxiety. "We'll continue to survey the house for more paranormal evidence. I've read that when a subject from our dimension transposes to another, there's a short period of time when the veil between both worlds is very thin."

"Sounds like horseshit to me," Larsa says, inadvertently tweaking a nipple.

"Yeah," Roxy edges in. "A veil? What the fuck are you talking about?"

Larsa smiles. "Sounds like something you just made up."

Ryan scowls at them both. "Great. That's the difference between you and me. When you two are fussing over your cinnamon dolce frappes with honey almond milk at Starbucks and blowing hours putting selfies on Facebook, I'm reading every scholarly article available on paranormal science, and it just so happens that there *is* a veil that exists between the various planes of existence—"

Roxy rolls her eyes. "You got enough bullshit in you to fill a fuckin' Olympic sized pool—"

"—and there's a name for it," Ryan continues. "It's called the Agnesi Membrane. Maria Agnesi was a theoretical physicist in the 1700s, and she discovered formulae, based on the work of Isaac Newton, that proved the functionality of strings of multiple universes and parallel dimensions. All you gotta do is look at the calculus."

Roxy grins sarcastically, nodding. "Oh, sure, Ryan, we'll be doing that. Right away!"

"Yeah," Larsa pitches in. "We'll be sure to check the *calculus!*"

Ryan disregards her. "The Agnesi Membrane can be feet thick while in stasis. But right after an energy transfer—like, for instance, a human making an ingression from this world to another place—that membrane can shrink all the way down to a thickness of one millimeter."

"Ingression," Larsa says. "That's super, Ryan. Wow, you're so smart!"

"Yeah," Roxy hastens to add. "Yeah, and this conversation is more boring than watching paint dry."

Ryan glowers, getting mad. "You two dunces can think what you want, but remember, *I'm* the boss, and if you want your cut of the money, you'll do what I tell you!"

Roxy and Larsa look at each other.

"You know," Roxy points out. "The two of us together could give him a serious beat-down."

"I was thinking the same thing," Larsa mentions. "But, fuck. What if Amy really does find money over there?"

"After all this shit, I'd want my fucking cut," Roxy says.

Larsa's nipples harden for no good reason. "So, if that dipshit never comes back and there's no money—"

"—*then* we'll beat Ryan's ass black and blue," Roxy guarantees. "We'll hang him upside down by his nuts and see how long it takes for his ball-sack to snap."

Ryan gulps.

"Okay, Ryan," Roxy consents. "You wanna be the boss, fine. You're the boss. Tell us what to do."

"The, uh, intelligent thing," Ryan says. "First, let's record some footage in infrared and see that we get."

Roxy and Larsa follow Ryan down the stairs. As he passes out the camcorders, Larsa looks distraught.

"Damn," she says thoughtfully. "For all the times I've bitch-slapped Amy and called her a sperm canoe and a cum dumpster … I sure hope she's okay …"

Amid spangles of throbbing purple light and weird geometric cross-hatches of multicolored lines of luminescence, Amy steps out of the shower, screaming.

She looks at her own hands, then looks at herself in the mirror. All of her skin is in place. She checks her body over just to make sure.

"Fuck me …"

The Parallel Dimension looks spectacularly different, like a negative filter. Amy realizes at once that she's in a house identical to the Marsten House, only its polarity is reversed.

Pulse racing, she grabs a towel off the rack and

wraps it around herself.

"This is fucked-up!"

Very slowly, she peeks out of the bathroom, fretfully looking both ways down the hall. Everything throbs and shimmers in kaleidoscopic and insane colors.

Amy hesitates, confused and unsure of herself. "What the fuck am I supposed to do?" she whispers. "Where am I gonna find this money?"

She takes the plastic bag from around her neck and opens it to remove the phone.

She dials Ryan's number, listens, looks at the screen, and frowns.

"Shit! No connection. But I guess it can't hurt to—"

She shoots a few pics with her phone: the hallway, the stairs. Then she moves downstairs and shoots still more pictures. Attaching them to a text, she presses the SEND button.

Entering the kitchen, she muses, "I wonder if there's any beer in this freakshow place …"

She opens the fridge and leans over, elucidating her ass.

It's a *great* ass …

"Fuck," she mumbles.

The fridge is empty.

"Figures. Nothing. I guess you don't have to eat or drink in another dimension …"

When she closes the fridge door, a glowing, shifting superimposition of Asenath Marsten is standing in an area of space that had been empty before.

Asenath grins evilly. Asenath is just as, if not

more, endowed of bosom as Amy. Threads of electrical energy crackle around her.

"Hello, Amy. How nice of you to stop by," Asenath greets.

Amy screams at the top of her lungs.

Ryan, Roxy, and Larsa are mounting the stairs with their handicams when Roxy stops short.

"Did you hear that!?" she exclaims.

Larsa's eyes shoot wide. "I think I *did* hear something, like a very distant—"

"—scream!" Roxy finishes, unnerved yet exited. "And it kind of sounded like—"

"I think I heard it too," Ryan admits, "and it did sound like Amy's voice ..." He puts his ear to the wall on the side of the stairs. "Is about here where it came from?"

"Yeah!" Roxy says.

"So it proves that the Agnesi Membrane is super, super thin right now." Ryan faces the wall and shouts, "Amy! Can you hear me?!"

He presses his ear to the wall again.

"Anything?" Larsa asks.

Ryan's face scrinches up in frustration. "I think so, but it was too faint to make out any details. Turn on your cameras. Maybe on infrared, we'll be able to see fluctuations in the membrane's thickness."

When he turns off the hall lights, the walls are very faintly traced by a strange luminescence.

"Shit! See what I mean?" Ryan blurts. "The membrane's so thin, light from over there is seeping over here!"

They all turn their cameras on in the faint light, then slowly move forward. Suddenly, Larsa's eyes bug and she jumps, shocked—

"Fuck me!"

She spins and looks behind her but sees nothing, yet five fingernail marks have appeared on her right buttock.

Ryan looks down the hall with his infrared. "You gotta be shitting me!" he yells.

He sees this very plainly in the infrared viewfinder: a luminous superimposed arm extends from the wall, sinking long, elegant fingernails into Larsa's butt-meat.

Roxy screams when she looks in her own viewfinder: many more luminous arms are churning out of the walls.

A melee breaks loose. Several hands catch Roxy's wrists, Larsa's ass, and Ryan's neck. The three of them struggle against the spectral limbs as they are battered and molested.

Somehow keeping hold of their cameras, they manage to grab onto each other and extricate themselves from the mass of otherworldly attackers. Then they scramble.

"Go!" Ryan yells. "Run fast; don't let them touch you!"

They hurtle downstairs, running a final gauntlet through the flurry of scrabbling luminous arms. They arrive, safely and exhausted, in the living room, but Ryan takes a fearful glance back upstairs. There, embossed into the wall at the top, the glowing, grinning face of Asenath Marsten radiates, electricity surrounding her.

"This is fucked-up, Ryan!" Roxy cries.

"And it's your fault! Let's leave!" Larsa adds.

"We *can't* leave!" Ryan shouts. "This is the first proof in human history of a parallel universe!" As he is about to argue further, his cellphone plinks. He looks at the screen and nearly shits his pants. "Unbelievable! Amy just texted me pics from the other side!"

They all crowd together, looking at Ryan's phone. Various phone pix pop up: the bathroom, hallways, the kitchens, etc., but they're all glowing in weird colors. The last pic is a selfie of Amy doing a duckface.

Ryan slumps down on the couch, frustrated. "Shit! I gotta think! Amy's life depends on it!"

Roxy wanders over to the wall and puts her ear to it.

"I wouldn't get too close," Ryan warns, "because—"

In a split-second, a woman's luminous foot slips out of the wall and—*FWAP!*—kicks Roxy hard right between the legs. She grunts, grabs her crotch, and falls over.

"Fuck!" she wails. "That's the third time today I've gotten kicked in the cunt!"

"I told you to stay away from the wall!" Ryan reminds her.

Larsa laughs heartily at Roxy, but her expression changes to one of shock as two luminous hands shoot out of the wall, turn her around, and yank her face-first against it. There's a loud chunky *KURRR-HOCK!* Larsa stumbles backward. Mortified, she spits onto the floor.

"Eww, gross! Some ghost-bitch just hocked in my mouth! Yuck!"

Ryan wrings his hands. "Come on, girls. We gotta brainstorm. Help me think!"

Meanwhile, in the paradimensional living room, Amy shivers. The luminous Asenath sits before her, grandiose tits sticking out. Standing opposite are seven more women, all attractive and stark naked, tinged in kaleidoscopic light. One of them grins with especial gusto: April Russo, her tits likely the best of the bunch.

"Say hello to my entourage, Amy," Asenath says coyly.

Amy is terrified. "What are you gonna do? Kill me?"

"Don't be silly, darling," Asenath says dismissively. "Why would we do that? If you want to know the truth, all we want you to do is leave. Go back to your own dimension. Nine's a crowd."

This information astonishes Amy. "How do I get back? The shower?"

"There's not enough energy for the transference," Asenath tells her, "so we have to harness some. In fact—" She reaches behind the couch and pulls out a suitcase. She opens it and shows Amy what's inside.

"Holy fuckbucket!" Amy exclaims. The suitcase is full of banded cash. "The million dollars!"

"Yes, and it's all yours to take," Asenath grants. "But first, you have to increase the energy threshold over there before you can leave here."

Amy squints. "How the hell do I do that?"

"Simple, dear." Asenath smiles genuinely. "Just listen to me and do exactly as I instruct …"

In the *other* living room, Ryan, Larsa, and Roxy are stewing over possibilities of what to do but coming up with nothing.

Ryan's phone plips again. He looks at it. "Damn! Amy just texted another pic; check this out!"

Roxy and Larsa both lean their fabulous bare breasts toward Ryan. He is *sandwiched* by fabulous bare breasts.

On Ryan's phone is a pic of a very luminous Amy, holding up a card on which is written: OUIJA BOARD!

"Of course!" Ryan exclaims. "Why didn't I think of that? Come on! Larsa, you're the Ouija board again!"

"Aw, fuck," Larsa replies, her lack of enthusiasm more than apparent.

Ryan positions her on the floor and puts more black stick-on letters on her belly. He opens a beer, chugs it, then takes up the beer cap. Giving Roxy a pad and a pen, he kneels at Larsa's left side. He puts a fingertip in the bottlecap.

"Amy!" he announces. "Amy! Are you there?"

The bottlecap shoots to YES.

"How can you get back here?"

The bottlecap jerks back and forth.

Roxy interprets. "She said, 'Need more energy from your side. Must be synaptic energy.'" She looks confused. "What the fuck's synaptic energy?"

"Energy generated from the brain," Ryan explains, "through electrical activity between brain cells. It's at its strongest with strong emotions like fear, rage, lust—"

The bottlecap moves around again.

Roxy's brows shoot up. "You'll love this, Ryan. She just said, 'The equipment in the attic is still turned on but energy must be boosted. You three must have mongo sex. Your orgasms will make enough energy for me to come back.'"

Ryan grins. "Looks like you girls get your wish. Get ready for Mr. Meat Missile!"

Roxy also grins. "I'm game for a good boning, that's for sure!"

"Ryan, with a salami like yours?" Larsa says. "You can do me till I pass out!"

Ryan is all smiles. "Okay, Amy! We're starting now, so get ready!"

The bottlecap slides rapidly. Roxy laughs. "She said, 'Lay some pipe on those bitches! Bang them both so hard they'll be sucking their thumbs and crying for their mommies!'"

Ryan, quite full of himself, stands up. "Okay, girls. Time for you to meet the Dick of the Apocalypse ... To the attic!"

The three of them excitedly ascend, assembling in the attic, where the shelves of electronic equipment are blinking manically.

Ryan, stripping naked as the statue of David—only with a much bigger dick—is, as usual, spewing presumed knowledge. "In this close proximity to the equipment, the veil is thinner than ever up here. The perfect location for an effective transfer of synaptic energy, wouldn't you say?"

But all that he says is ignored. His erection is the size of a tennis ball can. Roxy and Larsa are standing slack-jawed.

"Fuck!" Roxy blurts. "We only saw it limp. But this … this—"

"Is the biggest boner I've ever seen in my life," Larsa reveals.

Roxy's eyes sparkle. "Full mast! You could bounce it like a fuckin' diving board!"

"So big I'll need a damn shoe-horn …"

"Oh, bullshit, Larsa. You cooter's so stretched out you could park a city bus in it and you wouldn't feel a thing."

Larsa wags a stern finger at her. "Don't *make* me plunger your pussy like a gas station toilet."

Roxy does a *Bring It On* gesture with her hands. "Come and get it, dick-cheese face! I'll wear you out."

They're about to start fighting, but Ryan, annoyed, breaks it up. "Stop this nonsense, you two! We've got serious banging to do!"

Larsa and Roxy cool off, remembering their priority. "Yeah. We gotta get Amy back," Larsa says.

Ryan gestures to the floor. "Ladies? Shall we?"

The hot-to-trot trio waste no time getting down onto the floor, nor does Ryan's John Holmes-sized erection waste time burrowing into the well-used vaginal barrels of Roxy and Larsa. What commences after that is a scalding Adrian Lyne-type sex scene, including no small amount of lesbianism …

The gear and scientific equipment in the room

hums and revs, and the equipment lights blink faster and more furiously. The action is so hot that the interdimensional light starts to throb more overtly, into the room and over the entwined bodies.

As Ryan, Roxy, and Larsa all begin to shriek in a cannonade of orgasmic bliss—

Amy and Asenath are in the glowing bathroom on the other side of the veil. The weird light in the room fluctuates faster, and the meld of colors throb brighter.

Asenath seems pleased with the steady surge of power. "I'm impressed. That boy is really putting the blocks to those floozies. Their lust and desire is so off the hook, it's tripled the available energy."

But Amy frowns. "Those lucky douchebags. I could go for some of that action myself. Fuck!"

"You can have all that and more," Asenath promises, "once you get out of here. No offense, Amy, but you need to go. This is *my* domain. I don't like competition."

Amy is elated at the insinuation. "Really? You think I'm *that* hot?"

"Uh, well," Asenath falters. "But now it's time for you to return whence you came. You know the drill."

Amy drops her towel, turns on the shower. The shower spray is all exotic sparkling colors. She picks up the suitcase full of money, steps into the shower, and turns to Asenath.

"Nice meeting you ..."

And then Amy's flesh begins to melt as the energy increases. Through gritted teeth, she grins at Asenath.

The paradimensional lights go crazy, then—

Amy rips apart and disappears.

Meanwhile, back in the attic, Ryan, Roxy, and Larsa sprawl exhausted on the floor, covered with flesh-colored slime and lumps of plasma.

"Holy moly," Ryan mutters. "You girls wore me out."

Larsa turns and groans. "Fuck, I feel like I got run over by a steamroller."

Roxy lolls back; her eyes roll in her head, and she's grinning sheepishly. "Ryan's a stud-muffin. I came like a freight train."

Then Larsa looks nauseated; she's scraping the flesh-colored slop off her body. "Gross! What's with all this yucky shit?"

"I suspect it's plasmotic effluent," Ryan says. "The result of air molecules from this dimension coming into contact with air molecules from the *other* dimension." He distastefully flips the plasm off his body, then puts his clothes back on.

They all look up, hearing footsteps tramping up the stairs and then up the ladder to the attic. A shadow courses over them …

"Amy!" Roxy shouts with glee. "You're back!"

Ryan is about to have a cow. "This is the greatest achievement in paranormal science, and we've got it all on camera!"

"It worked!" Larsa celebrates.

Amy wipes the slop off her shining body with her towel, then drops it to the floor with a *splat!* Her body glimmers like a flesh-colored gem. She's still holding the suitcase. "It worked big time! And I owe it all to Asenath. She's not the bitch we thought. She told me exactly what to tell you on the board. And she even gave me the money!"

She opens the suitcase, revealing that it's stuffed with banded hundred-dollar bills.

Ryan, Larsa, and Roxy go apeshit.

"It was all true!" Larsa shrieks.

"We're set for life!" Roxy cheers, bug-eyed.

Ryan is giddy like a kid at Christmas. "And I'll write a thesis on paradimensional science, backed up with photographic documentation! We'll all be famous! Netflix will do a series on us!"

Amy is out of breath with excitement. "I can move out of my shitty trailer and live in a good place!"

Roxy nods vigorously. "I won't need a food card anymore … but I'll keep it anyway. Fuck the government."

They laugh and head to the stairs.

In the living room, Ryan, Roxy, Larsa, and Amy all come together in a group hug, overjoyed. Then they just stare a while at the suitcase full of cash.

"Come on, girls," Ryan finally says. "Mission accomplished! It's time for us to get—"

"—the FUCK out of this fucked-up house!" Amy finishes, all wreathed in smiles.

Awesome hanging boobs and preeminent

jutting butts show in paramount fashion as they bend over and start putting their regular street clothes on.

Suddenly, they stiffen up and hold their heads, wincing.

From out of nowhere, a low-pitched eerie tone resounds all around them.

Larsa grimaces in pain. "It's like a drill in my head!"

"What's the damn noise?" Roxy groans, grinding her teeth.

But Ryan has a look of dread on his face. "Oh, no … I think … look!" He points up the stairs.

It's like a dramatic reveal in a movie …

Standing at the top are Asenath, April, and six other spectacularly naked women, all shining in a sheen of flesh-colored slop.

"Holy fuck!" Larsa shouts. "It's an invasion from the other dimension!"

Asenath's grin radiates, and so do her eyes—a throbbing, shifting purple. "It sure is, you ridiculous bar tramp!"

"You lied to me!" Amy cries, outraged.

"Of course I did," Asenath gloats, "and you fell for it. Looks like when God was passing out brains, you were standing in the tit-line."

"Great job, Amy," Larsa gripes. "You brought them right to us."

"Fuck you!" Amy blathers.

"Shut up!" Ryan yells. "Run!"

They rush to the front door. An electrical discharge crackles across it.

"Open the fuckin' door, Ryan!" Roxy snaps.

Ryan is frantic, jiggling the knob. "It's locked! The knob won't even turn!"

By now, Asenath and her entourage are downstairs, surrounding Ryan, Amy, Larsa, and Roxy. All the intruding women possess the same luminous-purple eyes as Asenath; even their teeth are like tiny purple lights in their mouths.

"I control the house now, Ryan," Asenath announces. "With my mind. Being on the other side magnifies our psychic power, and it gives us superhuman strength."

"Terrific," Ryan says.

April Russo steps forward and demonstrates by effortlessly punching a hole in the wall.

Asenath smiles haughtily at Amy. "Did you really think I *wanted* to stay over there? Stupid, brain-dead …"

Amy glares back. "You evil cuntisaurus!"

"April," Asenath directs, "secure our money, please."

April Russo's boobs swing grandly as she closes the suitcase and takes it.

"And now, girls?" Asenath pauses for effect. "Let's fuck these ass-hats *all up!*"

But all at once, the entire house *shudders* as if wracked by a temblor. Everyone is sent staggering this way and that. All those bare boobs wobbling prove a satisfying sight.

"What the fuck!" someone shouts. "An earthquake!"

But it's *not* an earthquake …

A deep, reverberant voice emanates from all directions.

"NOOOOOOOOO!"

A dark, shrouded figure materializes in the center of the room.

Ryan and the three girls with him fall backward. They are terrified at this new apparition that has come between them and Asenath. Ryan, in fact, may have peed his pants …

Asenath and the Evil Naked Girls have regained their footing, while Asenath herself squints quizzically at the swirling, luminous manifestation.

"YOU SHALL NOT HARM THEM!" the voice booms. "BEGONE, FOUL CREATURES! BEGONE FROM THIS DIMENSION!"

The specter raises its arms menacingly.

"Septimus?" Asenath inquires.

"BEGONE, VILE WOMAN! YOU WILL NOT HAVE THESE YOUNG PEOPLE, OR THIS HOME!"

Asenath steps forward, glaring, and the specter steps back.

"You cheap old dangler!" Asenath laughs. "You no-fucking, no-boner tightwad old fuck!" She takes a crackling purple swipe at the vaporous shape that is Septimus Marsten.

"DON'T YOU DARE TRY MY PATIENCE! YOU HAVE NO IDEA OF THE POWER I POSSES!"

"Try this on for some power, asshole!" Asenath's hand shoots a coursing electrical discharge at the form of Septimus, who's thrown back against the wall.

He howls with a tenor that makes the house vibrate, and then his voice loses its thunder. "Damn it! Shit fuck piss!"

"Power, huh?" Asenath chuckles. "Where?"

Septimus feebly responds, "I tried to scare these nitwits out of the house because I *knew* you were up to something. They may be nitwits, but they don't deserve to be thrown into your meat grinder just for your obscene pleasure!"

"Sure they do. People this ridiculous have no right to live," Asenath retorts. "Great tits? Sure. But that's about it. They're all dumber than a box of used rubbers."

Amy pouts. "Hey, that isn't nice ..."

April Russo strides right up to Amy and—FWAP!—delivers a high sweeping side-kick across Amy's breasts. Amy *thunks* to the floor.

"Nice enough for ya?" April quips.

"Right in the knockers!" Asenath celebrates and claps her hands. Then she redirects her attention back to the withering Septimus. "We've been working on this a long time ... ever since I killed you! I just never counted on getting pulled into that goddamn dimension myself!"

Septimus takes a fighting stance. "Maybe this group of idiots isn't worth saving, but I must protect the Earth from you and your band of hussies! I am a scientist! I have studied the mystic arts from beyond the grave in order to stop you, Asenath! My powers are more than mortal! Even more than your interdimensional strength, speed, dexterity, and sexual allure! I will vanquish you and protect the world, and this will finally allow me to rest. My discoveries will change the world for the better. You see, the quantum intricacies necessary for perfect spatial transposition between dimensions is wholly predicated on …"

As Septimus prattles on, Ryan and his companions slowly get sleepy. Roxy actually nods off. Asenath checks her nails and takes a seat; she is yawning. The Evil Girls and April also begin to nod off.

"Jeez, you're *boring as fuck,* Septimus," Asenath complains. "Your jibber-jabbering is putting us all to sleep! Boring as fuck in life, boring as fuck in death."

She lets a jolt of purple electricity fly from her hands and whips it back and forth across her platoon of Evil Girls. The girls all rouse and wake up.

"Girls," Asenath announces. "It's time to kick ass!"

The Evil Girls are throbbing now in a fine mist of purple light; Ryan, Amy, Roxy, and Larsa all wake up as well. They rise as if to do battle.

Septimus laughs. "You already killed me once; you can't do it again! I'm a ghost! You can't kill what's already dead!"

"You sure about that, Professor?" Asenath asks, grinning, "You're sure you're no longer a corporeal being?"

"I'm certain of it!" Septimus snaps back.

The Evil Girls converge and grab onto him.

He is shocked. "But … but … I'm a ghost! You shouldn't be able to do this!"

"A ghost, yeah," Asenath replies, "but in which dimension? The Agnesi Membrane applies to you too, *Professor*. Ladies?"

Asenath's crew of grinning women each grab

a limb and draw Septimus out. April Russo approaches with a smile …

"You know what to do, April," Asenath says.

April traipses behind Septimus, then teasingly inserts her hand into his rectum.

Septimus bellows.

"How's this sound, Professor?" Asenath says. "She's gonna pull your Good & Plenty-sized dick out your ass …"

More hoarse bellowing ensues, making not a bit of sense, until the task is accomplished. In an organic presentation that exists beyond the spectacular, Septimus's scrotum and "Good & Plenty-sized" penis now hang prolapsed from his outraged anus.

Ryan, Roxy, Larsa, and Amy all look on in horror.

"Holy shit!" Larsa exclaims. "She pulled his dick *out of his asshole!*"

Asenath nods with thinned eyes. "Pretty creative, huh?"

One of her other very endowed cohorts speedily cuts Septimus's throat and drops him to the floor, spurts of blood spewing out with such fervor it eerily whistles.

Then Asenath's sly glance swerves to Ryan. "And now … What to do about you?"

"Oh, please don't rush!" Ryan babbles. "I'm in no hurry!"

As he and the girls scatter, trying to get away, Roxy's, Larsa's, and Amy's boobs all wobble impressively.

"I'm bored already," Asenath says. "Finish

these losers off so we can get out of here …"

One girl with skull tattoos digs her hands into Larsa's face, then pulls the whole thing off like a stocking mask. Larsa's mouth continues to open and close as she gurgles and dies.

Two more of Asenath's girls hold Amy's arms out, while another, with heart-shaped tattoos on her nipples, kneels and slips a hand all the way up Amy's vagina. The hand rummages around as Amy shrieks, then comes back out, holding two meatball-like ovaries.

The ovaries are held up, dangling from scarlet fingers. "You can wear these for earrings!"

Amy's vagina pours blood like a walrus projectile-vomiting chum …

"Better wash your hands," Asenath advises. "Don't want to get monkey-pox."

Amy convulses on the floor in hitching death throes, while Ryan liberally urinates in his pants.

Now it's Roxy's turn.

Several more of Asenath's girls surround Roxy. One promises, "I'm gonna ride your face like a bicycle seat!"

"Stay away from me!" Roxy yells, "you paradimensional bean-flicker!"

Another accomplice steps right up and—

FWAP!

—kicks Roxy in the pussy. This time, the foot caves in her pelvic cavity and buries itself in her abdomen. There's a sound like crunching pretzels.

Roxy grunts, "Ugh, fuck," then collapses. "That's the fourth time today I've gotten kicked in the cunt!" she complains as she dies, hiccupping blood and grue.

The girl who'd kicked her has trouble extracting her foot from Roxy's corpse. "It's stuck!" she blares, yanking.

April Russo's big tits wobble when she strides confidently up, steps down on Roxy's face, and heaves on the foot-stuck girl's leg until—

SCHLUP!

—the foot comes out. Then, as a neat flourish, April stomps hard on Roxy's head, crushing it to a mishmash of gore.

Yet another paradimensional girl—this one with a honker of a camel toe—slips behind Ryan and pulls his pants down to his knees.

Every one of Asenath's girls freeze where they stand, staring in disbelief at the sheer *size* of Ryan's Baloney Pony.

"Are you fuckin' shitting me?" one exclaims, gawping.

"Indeed, he's quite the man," Asenath says. "His cock is a masterpiece of organic perfection. Too bad we have to pull it off ..."

"No!" Ryan pleads. "I'm begging you! Not my John Thursday!"

"Seems a shame," another girl says, but then she shrugs, grabs Ryan's junk at the root, and—

"Ta-da!" Asenath celebrates.

—rips his cock and balls clean off, then heaves the whole works away, where it hits the wall with a bloody thud.

In all, the confrontation makes for an invigorating sight.

Ryan keels over to the floor, bellowing perhaps

louder than any man has *ever* bellowed, his groin gushing blood like a sludge pump until it trickles down and he dies.

One girl giggles, "I'm sure glad we don't have to clean up the mess!"

"Good job, ladies," Asenath compliments with a sweeping glance. "These losers are toast. And now it's time for us to be on our way."

She opens the front door to the teeming night and leads them out. The last is April Russo, carrying the suitcase.

One by one, they all disappear into the darkness …

Days later, a fine bright morning blossoms over the Marsten House, a picturesque vision until one takes into account the cluster of police cars parked out front, all with red and blue lights flashing.

Several grim-faced officers scrutinize the exterior. A young officer barges out of the front door with a delirious expression on his face. He bends over and spontaneously vomits into a large flower pot full of gardenias.

Inside, in the living room, the overweight, burned-out-looking police chief is holding a handkerchief to his face, looking nauseous. Dignazio, his sidekick, gags.

"Damn," the chief says. "Looks like someone went psycho bigtime. A regular Manson job."

Dignazio nods grimly. "This house has been nothing but trouble for decades. Somebody ought to knock it down. Fuck, I'll rent the bulldozer myself."

At their feet lay the bodies, three female, one male. One woman's tongue protrudes from her lipless mouth, her face removed, showing lidless staring eyeballs. Another's once-bonbon-sized nipples are bruised purple now, and holes have been punched into her chest. Her "cut" effuses some unmentionable organic goo, as if from a nasty yeast infection. A third, perhaps once the physical pride of the three, has big tits flattening in death like baggies full of pudding. No vestige remains of her head, just a pulpy mass of fly-buzzing brain-slop and chunks of cranium the size of bits of safety glass. The chief's brow does rise, however, when he glances inadvertently—or maybe not so inadvertently—at what is left of her, well, her pussy.

The last, the male, lies askew like a dropped G.I. Joe, with his pants down and a Lake Superior-sized pool of coagulated blood between his legs. His dead eyes and mouth gape wide open in a macabre exclamation.

"Shit, boss." Dignazio points to the corner at the discarded genitals.

"Fuck," the chief says. "I ought to staple that onto the end of mine. Then my wife might finally stop bitching …"

In all, the Marsten House has been turned into a slaughterhouse.

"And I thought I'd seen everything, for fuck's sake," the chief adds

Another cop, Sergeant Eliot, calls down from upstairs. "Hey, Chief. You better come up here."

The chief looks up, noting the frazzled expression on Eliot's face. "What is it? Please tell me it's not more dead bodies."

The paling Eliot replies, "Just … come up here …"

He and Dignazio mount the stairs and meet Eliot in the hallway. The attic ladder is down.

"Straker's up there now. He found something weird."

"I'm too fat to crawl up there!" the chief says. "What the fuck is it?"

PFC Straker's head appears in the attic opening, looking just as pale as Eliot. "Scientific equipment. Capacitors, resistors, gauges and shit."

The chief strokes his beardless chin. "Well, they say old man Marsten was a scientist of some kind."

Another cop, O'Reilly, leans out of the bathroom. "Check this out, boss."

They follow him to the shower, littered with gobs of some flesh-colored slop.

"The fuck's this?" O'Reilly asks, pointing to it. "And do you smell something funny?"

"Yeah," the chief replies. "A fuck-ton of dead pussy downstairs."

O'Reilly shakes his head. "No, I mean more like ozone or something? That smell like electric motors give off."

The chief sniffs noncommittally and shrugs. He probably does smell something out of the ordinary but doesn't want to think too much about it. "Seems like a regular bathroom to me."

O'Reilly squints again at the slop the shower. "Just … something weird about all this."

"Maybe the smell's from the equipment up in the attic," Dignazio ventures.

The chief harumphs. "Sure, maybe this, maybe that. Come on, we gotta call the M.E. and see what he has to say."

He and Dignazio tramp back down the stairs, leaving O'Reilly peering around the bathroom as if he senses something uncanny.

Suddenly, he is seized by a headache like nails going into his brain. Fringes of glowing purple mist effuse from the shower.

O'Reilly clamps his hands against his temples. "Mother*fuck*! That hurts!"

A low-pitched eerie hum wavers in the room, and the purple mist starts to crackle …

An overly large, rotten hand, complete with claws, shoots out of the shower wall, latches onto O'Reilly's throat, and pulls him in. He doesn't even have time to scream.

Then the hum stops, wads of flesh-colored glop appear on the shower floor, and Officer O'Reilly is never to be seen or heard from again.

WHO IS EDWARD LEE?

Edward Lee is the author of over 50 horror, fantasy, and sci-fi books, and dozens of short stories. He has also had comic scripts published by DC Comics, Verotik Inc., and Cemetery Dance. A great number of his novels have been reprinted in Germany, Poland, Italy, Romania, Japan, and other countries. He is a Bram Stoker Award Nominee; his Lovecraftian novel INNSWICH HORROR won the 2010 Vincent Price Award for Best Foreign Book (Austria), his novel WHITE TRASH GOTHIC won the 2018 Splatterpunk Award for Best Extreme Horror Novel, and in 2020 Lee won the JF Gonzalez Lifetime Achievement Award. In 2009, the movie version of his novella HEADER was released by Synapse Films. He lives in Seminole, Florida.

MORE BY EDWARD LEE

- The Bighead
- The Television
- The Dollhouse
- The Backwoods
- Wet Dreams of Dead Gods
- Czech Extreme

MORE FROM MADNESS HEART PRESS

- Squirming All the Way Up
- Ten Words for a Wicked Woman
- PINS
- Bound with Briars
- Blade Job
- Curse of the Ratman
- Lights Out
- Pure Hate
- Trip Chainsaw
- Whispers of the Dead Saint
- Howling of the Unfortunate Dead
- Kennel
- Thrust Into Battle
- The Reattachment
- ALL MEN ARE TRASH
- Warlock Infernal
- Infernal Queen
- Nympho Shark Fuck Frenzy
- Trench Mouth

www.ingramcontent.com/pod-product-compliance
Lightning Source LLC
Chambersburg PA
CBHW021344060726
47591CB00006B/2157

* 9 7 8 1 9 6 7 5 1 7 1 9 0 *